PA JINGLEBOB

and the Grabble Gang

Mary Arrigan   Korky Paul

For Conor and Marcella
M.A.

For Oliver David Solomon
K.P.

www.maryarrigan.com

EGMONT
We bring stories to life

First published in Great Britain 2005
by Egmont UK Ltd
239 Kensington High Street, London W8 6SA
Text copyright © Mary Arrigan 2005
Illustrations copyright © Korky Paul 2005
The author and illustrator have asserted their moral rights
Paperback ISBN 1 4052 0914 3
10 9 8 7 6 5 4 3 2 1
A CIP catalogue record for this title is available from the British Library
Printed in Singapore

Contents

Sissy Sheriff   5

Greedy Grabble   13

Grotty Gifts   18

Bye-bye Buckaroo?   25

Super-Duper Stew   30

Whopping Baddies   34

Red Bananas

SISSY SHERIFF

Jemima Jinglebob and her great big pa sat on the porch, rocking on their rocking chairs. They had just arrived home to Buckaroo after a holiday in a modern town with hard sidewalks, brick houses and pink ice cream. Pa was busy sharpening sticks with his big knife.

'Evenin', Sheriff,' said the Mayor as he
passed with Mrs Mayor on their way to the
Buckaroo Saloon for their afternoon drink of
Mrs Grace's homemade lemonade. Mrs
Mayor wore a new hat while her husband
sported a watch with a gold chain that
stretched right across his fat tummy. 'You
plannin' on catchin' some bears
with them thar spears?'

'Nope,' replied
Pa Jinglebob.

6

'Howdy, Sheriff,' said Cowboy Clarence on his way to have a shampoo and set. His new shirt was made of handpainted satin. 'You plannin' on huntin' down some bandits with them little spears?'

'Nope,' said Pa Jinglebob. 'I'm making new knittin' needles.'

7

'Oh, Pa,' groaned Jemima. Her pa was the biggest, toughest-looking bloke in these parts. He was as broad as a brick wall, hairier than a buffalo and had hands like shovels. But all Pa was interested in was knitting.

'You the sheriff?' a new voice asked.

'Nope,' said Pa, casting woolly stitches on to his new knitting needles.

'Yes, Pa. You are the sheriff,' said Jemima, thumping her father's big, hairy arm.

'Oh, er, yep,' said Pa Jinglebob, looking down at the owner of the new voice.

The stranger was dressed in a long, patched dress, a wide hat, and boots that looked like they'd walked right around the world. She put her hands on her hips and scowled. 'Knittin'?' she said. 'I ain't ever seen a knittin' sheriff. Come on, Hercules, we won't get any help here.'

'Hold on, Grandma Tendercorns,' said a small voice. A small, skinny boy came out from behind the lady's skirt. 'I told you this sheriff whops baddies. I heard it from Mo the mail-coachman.

He said . . .'

'Enough,' said the lady, pulling her hat down over her ears. 'I'd never trust a man with knittin' needles. Big sissy.'

'Excuse me, lady,' said Jemima, standing as tall as she could without falling over. 'Just who do you think you're calling a sissy? My pa whops baddies better than anyone in this whole world. Right, Pa?'

'One plain, one purl,' muttered Pa, as he started into a fair-isle cardie.

'PA!' yelled Jemima.

'Huh? Oh yeah, I do that too,' said Pa.

'What seems to be the problem?'

10

'It's Osbert J. Grabble,' said the small boy. 'Tell them, Grandma Tendercorns.'

The lady sighed and sat on the porch steps. 'Hercules is right,' she said. 'Osbert J. Grabble is trying to put me and Hercules off our land.'

'Can't do that,' said Pa, knitting in some red stitches to look good with the purple ones. 'Against the law that is.'

'I know it's against the law,' said Grandma. 'But he doesn't do law, this Osbert J. Grabble. He just does what he wants. And he wants our land.'

'You'd best come in, Mrs Tendercorns,' said Jemima.

Come in.

GREEDY GRABBLE

'So,' said Jemima. 'Tell us about this crook, Grabble.'

Grandma Tendercorns took a rolled-up paper from her pocket.

'I nicked that from Grabble's saddlebag,' said Hercules proudly.

Grandma Tendercorns spread the paper out on the table. It was a map of all the land for miles around. A red line was drawn right across it.

'See?' she said. 'This red line is a railway. He's going to build a railroad right through our land. He's offered us shiny shoes, nice frocks and hats . . .'

'And handpainted satin shirts and a clock with a chain,' added Hercules.

'As if we'd sell our land for that rubbish,' muttered Grandma. 'That land belonged to my Pappy Tendercorns, and his pappy and his pappy's pappy. And to think I gave that creep some of my Super-Duper rabbit stew.'

Pa Jinglebob leaned closer and squinted at the map. 'Why,' he said, 'that line also goes right through our town, Buckaroo, and the forest beside it.'

'It does?' exclaimed Grandma with surprise.

'There, can't you read?' said Jemima, stabbing the word 'Buckaroo' with her finger.

'Nope,' replied Grandma. 'Ain't no use for letters where we come from.'

'This is very serious indeed,' said Pa Jinglebob. 'This means that Grabble will try to buy out the town of Buckaroo.'

'Pa!' exclaimed Jemima. 'Frocks, clocks chained to tummies, handpainted satin shirts – I think he's already started!'

'Darn it,' said Pa Jinglebob. 'We should never have left town to go on that holiday. Make some notices, sweet Jemima. We need to call a meeting.'

'If we're not too late,' groaned Jemima.

GROTTY GIFTS

'Listen up, folks,' said Jemima later. The whole population of Buckaroo had gathered in Mr and Mrs Grace's saloon.

They were dressed in fancy clothes
and shiny shoes. Even Not-Nice-Nellie,
ex-bandit, who now had a cleaning business
in Buckaroo, sported new feather dusters in
her ex-six-gun holsters. Everyone was talking
at once, making a terrible racket.

'I SAID LISTEN!' yelled Jemima.
'MY PA HAS SOMETHING TO SAY.'

Pa knitted the last stitch and bit off the wool.

'Did you folks know that a man called Osbert J. Grabble is planning to build a railroad right here in Buckaroo?' he asked, spitting out a bit of woolly fuzz.

There was a noise of shuffling feet and everyone looked at their hands, the ceiling, their bellybuttons – anywhere except at Sheriff Pa Jinglebob. Nobody answered.

'Nice man, Mr Grabble,' said Cowboy Clarence, wiping the runny paint from his shirt off his arm.

There was a crack of breaking wood and someone fell to the floor. 'Ouch!'

Mr Grabble gave me those new wooden chairs for my saloon!

'You see, Sheriff,' said Mr Bones as he polished his new undertaker's hat and didn't notice the black ink that stuck to his forehead. 'While you were away he came and told us he was building a railroad near here that would make Buckaroo a rich town with hard sidewalks, brick buildings and pink ice cream.'

'Did he show you the plans?' asked Pa.

'Er, harummph,' began Mr Mayor. 'There was no need, Sheriff,' he said. 'He told us not to bother about the stupid words.'

'Silly wallies!' said Jemima. 'Show them the plans, Pa.'

When Pa held up the plans for all to see, there was a huge gasp.

'That . . . that railroad doesn't go *around* our town. It goes right THROUGH it!' said Mrs Mayor. **GASP!**

'That's right,' said Jemima. 'Looks like he intends to knock down the whole town and the forest.'

Crack! Four more people fell through the new chairs.

Just then the door burst open and a breathless cowboy came running in. 'It's him!' he cried. 'It's that nice Mr Grabble. He's heading this way with two of his men.'

'Eh, mebbe you'd, eh, hide the knittin',
Sheriff,' whispered Mr Mayor.

'Nope,' said Pa Jinglebob, tucking his
knitting under his arm and following
everyone as they rushed out to meet the man
who was about to take over Buckaroo.

BYE-BYE BUCKEROO?

Outside, the thundering of hooves got louder and from the middle of the dust cloud, a man with a wobbly belly, a shiny suit, and a cigar emerged.

'Afternoon, Mr Grabble!' said Mr Mayor, bowing so low his new breeches split. 'Tell the sheriff that you're not going to knock down our town.'

'Afraid so,' said Mr Grabble. 'This here town is right in the middle of my new railroad. But I'm a fair and decent man. I have a nice place all ready for you,' he went on, pointing towards the scrubby land beyond Buckaroo.

'But . . . but that's the desert,' spluttered Mr Mayor.

'Yep,' said Osbert J. Grabble. 'Lovely and warm. Lots of sunshine and heaps of sand for the children to play with.'

Everyone began talking at once.

'Ain't nothin'
anyone can do,'
laughed Mr Grabble.
'Especially a sissy
knittin' sheriff,' he
sniggered to his two
sidekicks. 'You all
signed these papers to say that I'd given you
those fancy clothes and stuff. What you really
did was sign away Buckaroo, the forest and
the Tendercorns Ranch.'

Grandma Tendercorns was outraged. 'You
tricked me! I thought I
was signing to say I
would never sign away
our ranch.'

'He can't take our
town, can he, Sheriff?'
asked Miss Brown.

'Yep,' said Pa, unrolling some white wool.

'WHAT!' everyone roared.

'If you signed your names and took stuff, then the town is his,' explained Pa.

'But we thought we were signing a thank you note,' groaned Mr Mayor. 'Nobody bothered to read the words.'

Mr Grabble sniggered again. 'Let's go, boys,' he said to his sidekicks. 'We'll be back tomorrow with our demolition gang to knock Buckaroo to dust. We'll be starting with that forest.'

With whoops and cheers, the trio disappeared over the hill.

SISSY SHERIFF!

Maybe we'll get him to knit some pretty covers for our hot water bottles.

SUPER-DUPER STEW

'We're finished,' groaned Mr Mayor.
'All is lost.'

'Looks like it,' said Pa Jinglebob. 'TWO
plain, one purl. And mebbe a bit of a twist.'

'Knitting!' muttered the townspeople,
switching their attention to Pa. 'We're
about to lose our town and you just sit
there knittin'.'

Mutter, mutter, grumble, grumble.

'Hold on there, people!' shouted Jemima. 'You greedy lot signed away the town in exchange for grotty gifts that are falling apart, and you have the nerve to blame my pa!'

'She has a point,' said Mr Bones.

'I'm angrier than a bear sittin' on a cactus,' muttered Not-Nice-Nellie, waving her new feather dusters. 'Why don't I just go after that varmint, me and my boys,' she nodded towards the team of ex-bandits who now helped her to run her cleaning business. 'We'll knock that oily grin off his face.'

'No rough stuff,' said Pa Jinglebob. 'Go home, everyone. Except for my Jemima, Grandma Tendercorns, Hercules and you, Miss Brown, ma'am.'

'Jemima, my sweet,' said Pa, as the people slunk away. 'You and Hercules get lots and lots of buttons. And, Miss Brown,' he went on, 'bring every kid in Buckaroo to the schoolhouse.'

'And what about me, Sheriff?' said Grandma Tendercorns.

'You'll make up one of your Super-Duper rabbit stews,' he said.

WHOPPING BADDIES

Next morning, many riders, all with mean faces, dirty boots and no manners, thundered into town.

Yee-ha!

35

'Call the sheriff,'
Mrs Grace ordered
her husband. He ran
to the schoolhouse.
'They've gone!' he
shouted. 'That
cowardly sheriff has
done a runner with all of our kids.'

'And some of our horses,'
added Cowboy Clarence,
flicking his gelled hair.

Osbert J. Grabble hooted
with laughter. 'Wise man,
your knittin' sheriff,' he said. 'He wouldn't

want to face the might
of Osbert J. Grabble and
his gang. Come on, boys.
There's a whole forest to
be knocked down.'

36

Jemima Jinglebob was standing at the edge of the forest. 'I wouldn't go in there, Mr Grabble,' she said. 'It's dark in that thar forest. And scary. You and your boys should be careful.'

'Scary?' laughed Osbert J. Grabble. 'Me and my boys don't scare, no siree.'

By now the people of Buckaroo had arrived on the scene.

Osbert J. Grabble frowned. 'Go find your sissy sheriff. Is he away knittin' some curtains for your new desert homes? Haw haw.'

His men picked up their axes and picnic hampers and ran into the forest, laughing like itchy hyenas.

'Might as well go home,' said Mrs Grace. 'While we still have homes to go to.'

'Sshhh,' said Jemima. 'Wait.'

'See here, little lady . . .' began Mrs Mayor. She broke off as there were terrified screams and yells coming from the forest.

HELP!

'I warned you,' said Jemima. 'Scary place that forest.'

HELP!

38

Suddenly Grabble's men appeared.
'Aaaaggghhh!' they cried. 'Help!'

'Huh!' cried Osbert J. Grabble. 'Git back in
that thar forest, you men.'

I ain't going back
in that place!

I want my mummy!

'Ghosts, Mr Grabble!'

'With hundreds of glittering eyes!'

'And fangs.'

'Riding monster tigers!'

Throwing down their axes and picnic hampers, the men jumped on their horses and disappeared in a cloud of dust.

'Come back!' roared Osbert J. Grabble. 'There's no such thing as ghosts.' He broke off as the shrieking and screeching from the dark forest grew closer. His horse reared up in fear. The paper with all the signatures of the people of Buckaroo fell from the saddlebag. Quick as a flash, Jemima snatched it.

Got it!

Suddenly a horde of horrific creatures were seen darting through the trees. Some of them, skeletons with white bones, were riding striped monsters. Others, with two heads and hundreds of shiny eyes and four waving arms, chased after them.

'You can keep your scary forest,' croaked Osbert J. Grabble. 'I'm off. Wait, boys. Don't leave me!'

As the terrifying creatures emerged, laughing and giggling, the people looked at them with amazement.

They're our kids!

Sure enough, some of the children were dressed in scary knitted outfits with lots of shiny buttons sewn on. Others, wearing plain and purl skeleton outfits, were riding horses which wore striped, woolly coats.

'That was fun,' laughed Hercules, throwing a fair-isle snake in the air.

'Well done, team,' said Pa Jinglebob as he and Miss Brown joined them.

Later on, at a party in the Buckaroo
Saloon, Mrs Grace planted a big kiss on Pa
Jinglebob's head. 'You've saved our town, Pa,'
she said.

'And the Tendercorns Ranch,' added
Hercules proudly.

'Not RANCH,' smiled Grandma
Tendercorns. 'COUNTRY RESTAURANT.
Mrs Grace here says my stew is the best darn
stew in the whole West, so me and Hercules
will be opening The Tendercorns Classy Nosh
House next week.'

Everyone cheered.

'We owe it all to our sheriff, Pa Jinglebob,' said Mr Grace.

'Shucks,' said Pa, blushing. 'It was the TWO plain, one purl and a bit of a twist that did it.'

'That's my pa,' said Jemima. 'Still the fastest knitter in the West.'